Little Princess

THIS BOOK BELONGS TO

_____

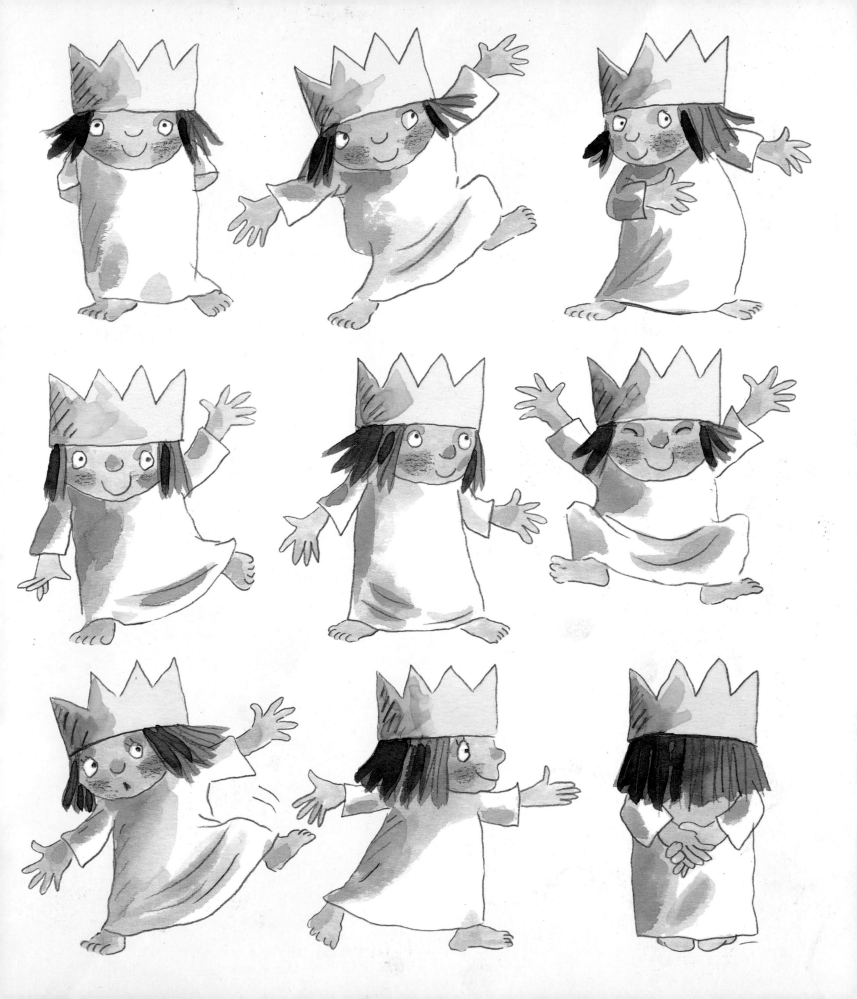

This paperback edition first published in 2017 by Andersen Press Ltd.

First published in Great Britain in 2010 by Andersen Press Ltd.,

20 Vauxhall Bridge Road, London SW1V 2SA.

Copyright © Tony Ross, 2010

The rights of Tony Ross to be identified as the author and illustrator

of this work have been asserted by him in accordance with the

Copyright, Designs and Patents Act, 1988.

All rights reserved.

Printed and bound in Malaysia.

1   3   5   7   9   10   8   6   4   2

British Library Cataloguing in Publication Data available.

ISBN 978 1 78344 600 1

Little Princess

I Want to Do it by Myself!

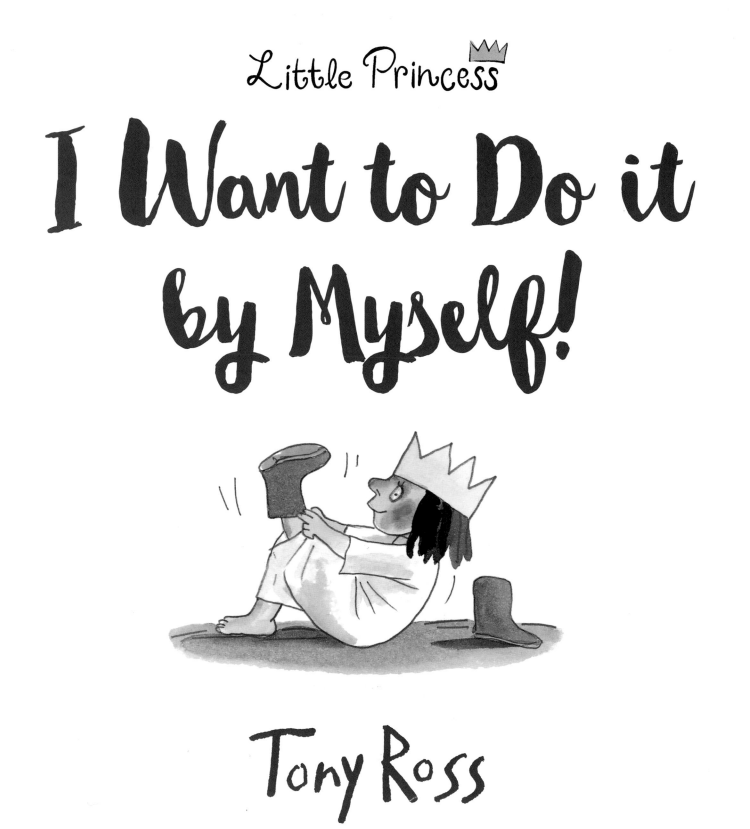

Tony Ross

Andersen Press

"Where are you going, Little Princess?" asked the King.
"I'm going camping," said the Little Princess.

"Let me carry your bags, then," said the Queen.
"No!" said the Little Princess. "I want to do it by myself!"

"You can go on my horse!" suggested the General.
"No!" said the Little Princess. "I want to do it by myself!"

"My boats will help to take your bags," said the Admiral.
"No!" said the Little Princess. "I want to do it by myself!"

And so, the Little Princess set off, all by herself...
... and soon found a beautiful place to camp.

But when she looked in her bags, she found that she
had forgotten to bring her tent.

So when the Little Princess went off to find something to use as a tent, the Prime Minister secretly set up his for her.

"Oh bother!" said the Little Princess when she returned.
"I must have brought a tent after all. I am SO forgetful.
I think I will make supper."

But when she looked in her bags, she found that she had forgotten a tin opener. She had forgotten a tin as well, so she went to look for something to eat.

While she was away, the Cook made a wonderful supper ready for her return. Although she could not remember making it, it was very tasty.

"Time for bed!" the Little Princess thought.
But she had forgotten a blanket and a pillow.
While she was away, looking for something to sleep on...

... the Maid made up a lovely camp bed.
"Oh BODDLE!" said the Little Princess. "I must
have forgotten I had that."

So the Little Princess tumbled into bed, and fell into a
happy sleep. She would have cuddled Gilbert,
if she had remembered to bring him.

In the morning, she looked in her bag for her towel and toothbrush, but she had forgotten to bring them.

Then she spotted them, under the bush.
"I must have put them there in my sleep!" she said.

After her wash, she sat down to think of something to do.

As there was NOTHING to do, the Little Princess
packed her bags again and set off home.

"Funny," she thought, "these bags seem heavier than they were yesterday. My stuff must have grown."

On the way back, she met the Gardener.
"Shall I help you with those heavy bags?" he said.

"NO, thanks!" said the Little Princess.
"I want to do it by myself!"

When she got home, everyone met her at the gate.
"How was your camping holiday?" they asked.

"It was WONDERFUL!" said the Little Princess.
"But I am tired now, because...

... I DID IT ALL BY MYSELF!"

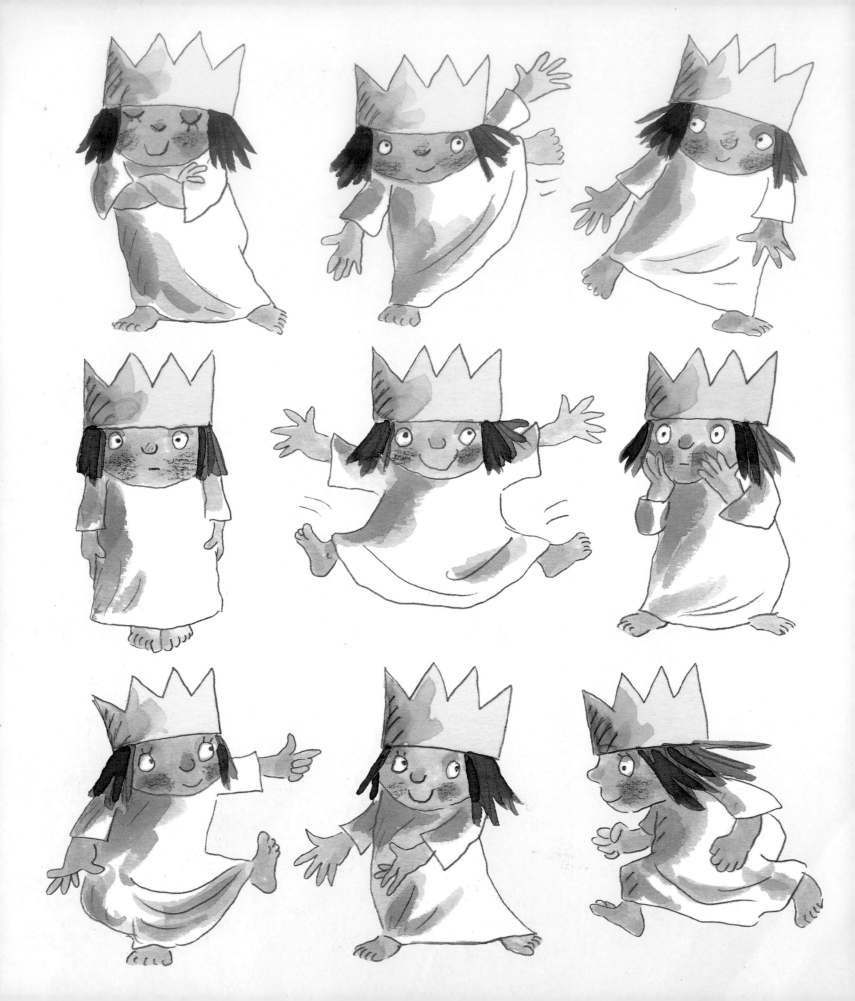